This Book Belongs To

Endorsements

"I have now read this book several times and have marveled at its unusual power. *The Winter Elf* can only be described as a masterpiece of children's literature. Grace Anne has created a one-of-a-kind tool for anyone who loves a child. And before the story even begins, the author's Letter to Grownups—a quick message to the book's likely narrators—has value well beyond the price of the book. Seriously."

—**Andy Andrews**, *New York Times* bestselling author of *The Traveler's Gift*, *The Noticer*, and creator of WisdomHarbour.com

"All good fairy stories show us who we are and help us to understand the world in which we live. As Tolkien says, they hold up a mirror, showing us ourselves. *The Winter Elf* is a very good fairy story. Charming and disarming, it takes us into an enchanted world so that we can see the pain and suffering of this world more clearly. It is a gift for suffering souls of all ages which edifies the troubled soul even as it heals the broken heart."

—**Joseph Pearce**, author of *Further Up and Further In: Understanding Narnia* and *Frodo's Journey: Discover the Hidden Meaning of The Lord of the Rings*

"As a child psychologist, this is now on my most recommended book list for parents to read to their children. *The Winter Elf* will delight and win fans. It is a winsome tale of healing which leaves the reader in a spirit of cherished reflection and loving comfort."

—**Dr. Trina Young Greer**, Psychologist,
Founder and Executive Director,
Genesis Counseling Center, Hampton, VA

"Grace Anne's love for children, fairy tales, and the deeper truths they convey shines through every page!"

—**Christin Ditchfield**, author of the best-selling
A Family Guide to Narnia

"*The Winter Elf* is a beautiful reminder that bringing our fears and hurts into the light means that the darkness no longer has the same power over us. As the wise elf shares his ancient saying, we all gain a solid reminder of the best way to bear a burden: by sharing it with those who love us. This story speaks to the hurting child in all of us with a message of redemption and healing."

—**Kim Nisbett**, Director,
Fine Linen Theatre, Rolla, MO

"At once both a moment in time and timeless, *The Winter Elf* is the best sort of fairy tale. Grace Anne's prose echoes the cadences and rhythms of Lewis, Potter and Dahl—clean, exact, and evocative—providing just the right touches of precise description to create that moment in time when her young hero Clara most needs guidance—and a gentle reminder that faith is a kind of magic, no less real merely because it defies explanation. Clara's journey is simple yet profound and will no doubt touch hearts and souls for many ages to come."

—**Dr. Daniel Reardon**, Associate Professor of English, Science Fiction & Fantasy Literature, *Missouri University of Science and Technology*

"A good story with a timeless message is hard to find but Grace Anne has conjured up a tale that will become a family favorite. *The Winter Elf* helps children understand they can learn and grow even when life seems harsh."

—**Joanne F Miller**, speaker, artist and author of *Creating a Haven of Peace, What If It Were Possible?* and *Be Your Finest Art*

"Grace Anne has achieved the enchanting task of what George MacDonald called inventing 'a little world of one's own.' Fans of fairytales will recognize her winter world, for it works a peculiar magic, making us long all the more for the good, the true, and the beautiful."

—**Andrew Lazo**, MA, editor of *Mere Christians: Inspiring Encounters with C.S. Lewis*, and of *Early Prose Joy,* Lewis's first spiritual autobiography

"Riddled with pithy wisdom, yet also woven into a rich storyline, *The Winter Elf* is sure to both inspire and challenge. It will no doubt become a favorite therapeutic resource for those who work with children, as it has all the elements of a classic. Highly recommended!"

—**Kenyon Knapp**, Ph.D, Dean, School of Behavioral Sciences, *Liberty University*

"Grace Anne succeeds in painting a stirring portrait of loss and pain by using a palette of friendship, compassion and hope, all on the canvas of a classic children's fable."

—**James Duke**, President, *Act One, Inc.*, Hollywood, CA

The Winter Elf

THE WINTER ELF

GRACE ANNE

NEW YORK

LONDON • NASHVILLE • MELBOURNE • VANCOUVER

The Winter Elf

Published in New York, New York, by Mount Tabor Media, an imprint of Morgan James Publishing. Morgan James is a trademark of Morgan James, LLC.
www.MorganJamesPublishing.com

ISBN 9781642795349 paperback
ISBN 9781642795356 case laminate
ISBN 9781642795363 eBook
Library of Congress Control Number: 2019937654

Cover Design by:
Megan Dillon
megan@creativeninjadesigns.com

Interior Design by:
Chris Treccani
www.3dogcreative.net

Cover design work by Drew.graphics
Photography by AlyssaJeanStudios.com

This book is dedicated to the thought of a child and kindred spirit who might cherish the story as much as I do. He or she has been my reason for writing from the beginning. I decided I never much cared if my books succeeded greatly, if only they reached this one soul. Thank you, dear heart.

Preface

This story has been a long time in coming. I have walked with these characters for years and learned more about them than could ever be written. At the same time, their lives are not my own, and they have several secrets they still wish to keep from me.

I hope my dear elf might bring some happiness to people, and provide a source of comfort and new understanding to aching hearts.

I have many memories of my father reading to my six siblings and me before bed as we lay scattered about the floor, eyelids growing heavy in the comfort of story time. Those nights instilled in me a wonderful sense of nostalgia, as enchanting characters and a passion for fiction were drawn up from my soul. These eventually found form in the tale before you now, which I invite you to enjoy and share in that same evocative spirit.

A Letter to Grownups

Dear Grownup,

Please seize this story as a chance to enter the world of childhood, fantasy, and even theatre. Storytime is not simply a means of lulling children to sleep but rather the duty to enrapture them in the imagination of another world and inspire the courage to follow dreams.

I am the author, but you are the magician. Cast a spell, then, with your voice, dim lighting, and perhaps a fire in the hearth or pine-scented candles. Create safety with hot cocoa, warm blankets, and a place for children to rest.

Enchant this story with a slightly slower and softer tone, as if there is a secret the children must wait to discover. Give voices to my Clara Rose and to my elf. Even try an English accent for Sydney; children don't much care if it's accurate.

Most importantly, dear grownup, if only for a moment, you must believe in magic. Believe in fairies and singing stars, in miracles and in elves. That which is improbable breeds the purest hope—the essence of dreams.

In storytime magic, the environment of fiction grows and merges with reality until dreams and imagination are indistinguishable. It is there that the world of fantasy turns out to be much more real than we pretend it to be.

So, capture the hearts of your little ones. Fill them with faith and wonder.

THE MOON SHONE LIKE DIAMONDS into the bedroom, casting mirroring shadows off the small child huddled against the foot of her bed. Hot tears pricked at her eyes as Clara Rose heaved slow breaths, hoping to silence her broken whimpering. Her dimpled hand lay at her side, fiddling with the loose button eye of her worn, stuffed bear. As another sob threatened the silence, the child lolled the back of her head against the footboard, causing her red hair to splay out across her face, redirecting her thoughts to the solid touch.

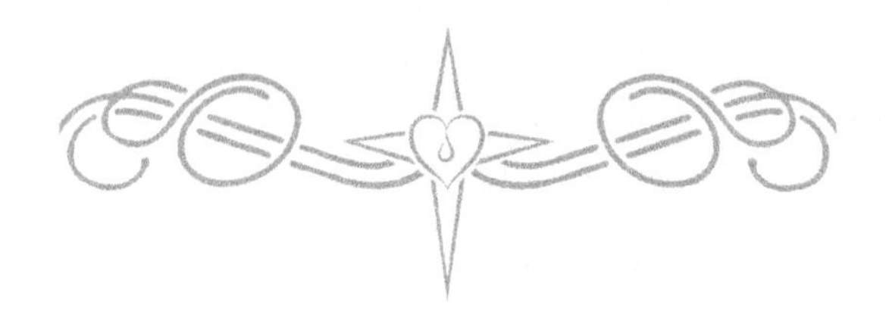

Her tears were interrupted as a sudden laughter broke out amid the mournful night. Clara Rose sat up with a start, poised as a rabbit as she listened for the sound. Just as she began to think she had only imagined the voice—it happened again! It was a single laugh but like a chorus of children playing by the brook on a summer's day. Clara Rose scrambled to her feet, tripping on the end of her nightgown as she scurried to the window.

Down on the snow-covered lawn was a man, though if not for his

height and white hair, he could have been mistaken for a young boy as he jumped and twirled about in the falling snow. He held a fedora in one hand, and over a fine suit he wore a long tan overcoat that flapped with every movement.

Clara turned from the window and hurried down the creaking stairs of the old colonial style home. Slipping into her coat and boots, she rushed to the door and heaved it open, letting in a gust of December air. The porch light illuminated the snowflakes dancing their way down

from the night sky. On the ground, snow was just beginning to pile up, now covering most of the grass.

All the night was still. It was a gentle kind of cold with no wind, and just enough chill to make one notice the warmth of their jacket. As Clara stepped onto the sidewalk, the snow crunched beneath her feet. On the lawn, she found the man now lying on his back and staring at the sky.

"Who are you?" the child asked, caution and curiosity fighting for control in her tone. The man gave a small gasp before flipping his heels

back over his head so that he was now standing.

"Clara Rose!" he shouted, an English accent playing hard on his tongue. A large grin spread across his young face as he bent to her height. "Here we are at last! I was hoping you'd come out."

"How do you know my name?"

The man's eyes popped open, "Oh, I suppose that does sound a little... odd. Well—I live back just a ways," he explained. "I saw when your parents first brought you home as a baby, and I've watched you growing

up, playing in the leaves with your friends, biking—ah! that little snow ramp you made with your dad was absolutely brilliant!"

"Oh," Clara responded, her eyebrows knitting together a moment. "Then why are you here now?"

The odd man straightened up with a gentle smile. "I know what you're going through and couldn't just leave you alone. You've got so much ahead of you. I'd hate to see it all snuffed out by a single moment in time."

Clara tilted her head as she began reading the strange man's features.

He was very skinny, and, despite his youthful appearance, he held an ancient air. His hair was what gave this impression more than anything, as the floppy cut was white as the gathering snow.

Beneath that were his eyes, a marvel which the child never forgot; both were the most striking green ever seen in an eye, but without notice they would change, seamless as a setting sun, becoming crystal blue or frosted grey instead.

On either side of his head, two large and rather pointed ears stuck out, all

the features now causing Clara's eyes to widen and her brow furrow.

"Who *are* you?" she insisted again.

The man perked up in an instant. "Oh! So sorry. My name is Sydney; Sydney Telson."

Clara leaned to one side and studied his ears again, "Are you—"

"An elf, yes," Sydney finished, fixing his hat back on his head. "Well, winter elf specifically. I think that's why the hair's white; snowflakes, stuff like that," he smiled.

"But—I thought elves weren't real."

"No, you did not!" Sydney's face wrinkled in offense before he dropped to her height, again lowering his voice to a whisper, "My dear Clara Rose, you practically believe in everything, and you certainly never stopped believing in elves. What is this? Why would you say something like that?"

"Because someone told me..."

"And you just let them?! Something pops out of someone's mouth, and you just believe it like that? Where is the Clara Rose who wouldn't have her dreams dashed so quickly?"

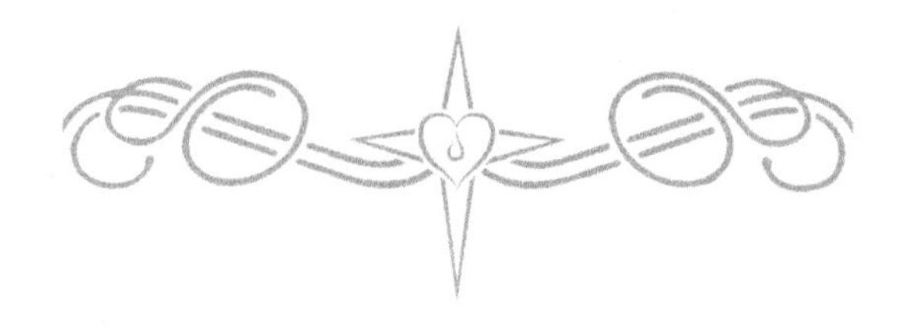

Clara turned, grumbling, "Nevermind. You wouldn't understand."

"Well I might," the elf called after her, straightening up. He shoved his hands into his trouser pockets and began talking to her back, "Your mum's been in hospital—for the past month. You never see her nor your daddy anymore, as he's always busy taking care of her. But with all that time he spends there, he never tells you what's going on. So you're left here to wonder; wonder and worry, and fear, and hope.

"Oh, you've got your sister, but you're not a great fan of her coping mechanisms. I know you've hidden underneath your bed a couple of times so she can't send you to clean the baseboards for the hundredth—"

"How do you know all this??" Clara demanded, spinning around.

"I told you. I've seen it happen. The time for waiting's over, and I've come to help."

"But why?"

Sydney gave a sad smile, bending down again, "Because you are loved,

Clara Rose, more than you can possibly fathom; that's why I'm here. You're not alone, but I think you've forgotten that."

He held out his gloved hand, "Now how 'bout it?"

Clara chewed her lip as she stared at the awaiting hand, "Will you fix everything?"

Sydney gave a small smile, "I'm afraid that's not my place to mess with, but I can help, and I think you could use some of that."

Sydney offered his hand again, and the two began to stroll across the great lawn and into the nearby wood. He led her under a little grove of pine trees, revealing the most magical sight Clara had ever imagined. Instead of the dirt and pine needles of a forest, they were inside a room, completely furnished with wooden floors and bookshelves in every corner. Loose sketches, hand tools, and an assortment of small clocks, only some of which were working, were scattered about the room in a captivating arrangement of orderly chaos.

Illuminating the room was a warm fire nestled inside an old hearth at the end of the living space. Shadows danced by the grace of the flames in all the nooks and crannies of the odd house, attempting to revive tales of a long-forgotten past. Above her head, the trunks and boughs of the trees could be seen hiding in the shadows and stretching up into the darkness where several winter birds flitted from branch to branch.

"Careful," the elf warned, calling Clara Rose from her reverie. "The

squirrels are sleeping. They get quite cross if you wake 'em up."

"Is this your house?" the little girl asked, moving her way towards the comfort of the fire and taking in every inch of the room.

"Well, I'm not sure if it even qualifies as a house, but it's home," he answered from the little kitchen opposite. "Oi, Sam, no making nests in the tea cups. How many times do I have to tell you?"

Clara turned from her musings to see a little red cardinal flutter up from his place in the china, chirping

and ruffling his feathers in a sort of indifference towards the elf. Sydney responded with a series of short whistles, promptly silencing the bird.

Clara Rose exclaimed, “You can talk to animals!”

“Yeah, ‘course I can,” answered Sydney, a twinkle in his eye. “What sort of an elf would I be if I couldn’t do that?”

In a few minutes, Clara found herself huddled in a blanket next to the crackling fire, a mug of hot cocoa in hand, while Sydney sat across in companionable silence.

He had removed his winter wraps and was now happily making cream mustaches with every sip of his cocoa. With a final drain of his cup, he set it gently on the ground and leaned forward over his crossed legs.

"So," he began, narrowing his eyes, "what happened to Clara Rose?"

Clara shifted under his deep gaze. "Well, you already know about my mom, and about my dad always being gone, and—" the child dared a glance at the elf, "I'm scared Mom might die. I'm lonely all the time, but it seems as if nobody cares."

She paused, and he waited. “Grownups keep saying that everything will be okay, but my friends told me that’s just a bunch of fairy tales to make me feel better.”

Sydney was quiet for some time, never breaking his caring gaze, but suspending her words in the silence.

Finally, he queried, “Do you believe in me?”

“What do you mean?”

“Well, elves are generally thought of as fairy tales, and you yourself said you didn’t think they were real—”

"Well, that's what everybody says…"

"What do you believe?" the elf pressed again.

Clara fell silent for a moment, her brow knitted in deep thought, "But won't I be made fun of if I believe in fairy tale stories?"

"Oh yes," Sydney replied in all seriousness. "Absolutely."

"Then why do it?"

Sydney leaned towards her, "Because you know I'm not a fairy tale. You know I'm real. But knowing something isn't the same as believing it. Believing

takes faith. So I ask you again, Clara Rose—what do you believe?"

Clara thought long and hard, trying to come up with as many options as she could. "Couldn't I just show you to people?"

Sydney chuckled, "No, belief doesn't work that way."

"Then how does it work?"

"You will learn over time," he smiled. "But! Know that when people do make fun of you, if you stand strong in what you believe, then you will come to understand better and you'll

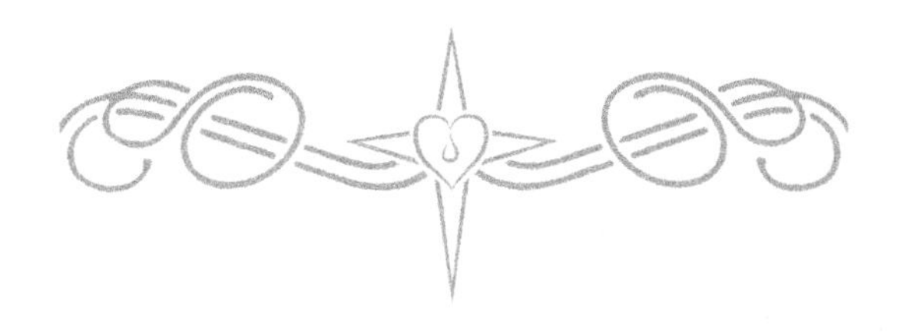

experience more of it. And your belief won't be for nothing. Some will listen and even be strengthened in their beliefs by the faith you have in yours; you just have to be patient and live it out each day."

Clara fixed her eyes on him, "You said you've known me this whole time?"

"I have. I've seen you playing with your friends, coming home from school, even running off to have a good cry."

The two fell silent as Clara Rose's face scrunched in deep thought. "How come I have to have everything the

hardest?" the girl pressed slowly, "It isn't fair!"

Sydney gave her the best smile he could muster. "I know it doesn't seem fair, but it's happening, and sometimes all we can do is decide who it will make us."

Sydney sat back, wondering at the little soul in admiration. "You're not just anyone, Clara Rose. You are going to grow a great deal through this. Painful pasts can make for the strongest futures if we let them. Remember, *Shah-yay, shah-yu, shah-yish.*"

"What?" interjected Clara Rose, a sudden puzzled look crossing her face at the gibberish.

"Sorry, it's an ancient saying the elves taught the humans ages ago, but the humans seem to have forgotten the words. In your language, it basically means share your heart, share your hurt, share your hope. I sometimes slip-up and say it in elvish: *Shah-yay, shah-yu, shah-yish.* These are the things that help us grow.

"Though the humans forgot the saying, I think it's why they whisper 'sh-sh-sh' when comforting each

other. They're not trying to shush anyone; they are *reminding* them."

With a smile, Sydney stood from his spot and moved towards a small crate in the corner behind her. "C'mere," he beckoned with a curl of his finger.

Following suit, Clara peered into the open crate and let out a delighted gasp, clearing away the dark thoughts for the moment. "You have a bunny!" she exclaimed, looking down at the creature snuggled in a ragged blanket.

Sydney smiled, watching as she began doting on the small animal. "Yeah. He got a bit knackered by a

dog the other day. I'm taking care of him. His name's Randall."

The elf knelt beside them, unwrapping a cloth of medical materials. He moved to peel old gauze from the rabbit's hind leg, and it began squirming under his touch. Sydney offered some soft squeaks and ticks of the tongue in response to a sudden wail from Randall.

Clara Rose muttered, "He doesn't seem to like it very much."

"Well of course he doesn't like it. It hurts. But it's the only way he'll get better." He turned back to the task,

but stopped himself short, "Tell you what, why don't you give it a go?"

"Oh, no. I would mess something up."

Sydney smiled, "Come on, I've seen you with animals before."

Switching positions, Clara gently peeled back at the bandage with one hand as she stroked the rabbit's head with the other. As she started to dab at the wound with a damp rag, Randall scurried to the other end of the crate.

"Talk to him," Sydney prompted.

Clara Rose began, speaking softly, "I know it hurts, Randall, but you need to trust me. I'll take good care of you, I promise. I can't make it better yet, but…you'll see; it'll be okay." The little girl caught Sydney's eye for a moment, then continued, "*Shah-yay, shah-yu, shah-yish.* Share your heart, share your hurt, share your hope," she soothed. "You'll get stronger as you heal, but you have to allow it to hurt for just a bit."

She gave him a little pat before setting back to her task. Randall still

twitched and trembled under her care, but the job was finished.

"Told you you could do it," said Sydney, glowing with pride. The child only smiled in response. Silence fell between the two, only interrupted later by Clara's heavy sigh. Sydney straightened and held out both his hands as she filled them with her own.

"You should be going home now. It's quite late. But listen closely, Clara Rose," Sydney whispered as he squatted down before her. "You have a lot of trouble to face ahead, but

be strong. Don't forget this night, especially when you feel alone. People are there all around you, and there is more love available to you than you can even begin to imagine. You won't be alone if you don't run from the good things you already know are there."

The elf paused, capturing the child with his impossible eyes of ancient youthfulness. "Do that, my dear, and you will be just splendid."

The jerking sensation of falling rushed over Clara, causing her to jump. She was forced to shut her eyes

when the unexpected white light of a December morning met her, instead of the warm crackling fire. At this sudden change, the small child sat up to find she was no longer in Sydney's cluttered living room but tucked in amongst the sheets of her own bed. There was no Sydney; not a trace of him anywhere.

Clara scrambled from the bed and began searching the room for any evidence of the mythical creature's presence from the night before. In her panic, she tried to send her mind back to the last words he spoke, the

last thing they did, but she couldn't focus. The memory was like a fading dream.

After an unsuccessful search, she crawled back onto the bed, fighting back tears as she resigned herself to the likelihood that it had all been nothing but a dream. What could she do? Must everything return to the way it was before, so lonely and hopeless?

Shah-yay, shah-yu, shah-yish. Share your heart, share your hurt, share your hope. The words sounded in Clara's head. She found herself repeating the

phrase, idly piecing together other bits of the conversation as the night came back to memory.

With a sudden start, she jumped again from the bed and ran to the window, hanging onto the fading idea before she lost hold of it altogether. There on the lawn, now half-covered in snow, were the scattered footprints and the imprint of his coated form from the night before. It had happened! She knew now she had to act to make good use of the elf's advice.

Clara Rose had to share what was inside her. She would go down this

morning and propose to her sister that they decorate for Christmas. Put aside the cleanup for one day and enjoy the comfort of each other's company as they cover the house in fond memories. Use the time to talk and connect over the worry of their mother's illness. The girls hadn't seen their mom in a long time; maybe Clara would ask to visit her again.

It wouldn't fix everything, she knew that, but it would make things better. It would help her grow and, as Sydney said, that's the important part of any situation. Sometimes that's enough.

The love was there and available, but it was up to her to allow it to heal her.

She would share her heart, share her hurt, and share her hope, and so pass through these shadows stronger and wiser.

The End.

About the Author

Grace Anne is an author, painter and musician who delights in exploring a wide range of emotional, relational, and spiritual experiences through the arts. Inspired especially by the fiction of CS Lewis and JRR Tolkien, she seeks to express "the good, the true and the beautiful."

(Continued)

She lives on her family's estate in the foothills of the Ozark Mountains of Missouri, where she loves meandering walks in the woods, soaking up the animals, and dreaming out under the stars.

You can follow her creativity on Instagram or Facebook: @GraceAnneOriginals

Or contact her on the web at: TheWinterElf.com

BRING THE STORY TO LIFE!

Visit **TheWinterElf.com** for your very own toy Randall and Sam, free downloadable coloring pages, and other treasures.

Acknowledgments

Special thanks to my father, Christopher, for encouraging and guiding me through this whole process, which took far longer and was far more work than I expected. This book would not be here without you.

Thank you to my mother, Rachel, and my siblings, Alyssa, Colin, Andrew, Sarah, Braden and Reagan, whose love and affirmation give me the confidence I often lack to share my heart.

Thank you to my grandparents, Ed and Mary Ann Kravos and Walt and Jean

McCluskey for your support in my journey and for the gift of your land to roam so I could write under the inspiration of nature.

Thanks to my fellow creative, Gracie Mentink, for your support and help during the editing process. You have the heart and integrity of a great author, my friend. May God bless you and all your work.

Finally, thanks to my technical team who've helped bring this dream to life: AlyssaJeanStudios.com for our tromping photo session in the woods, Drew. graphics for the gorgeous logo designs, FreshEyesInc.com for the stunning website, and Mount Tabor Media and Morgan James Publishing for the incredible guidance every step of the way. No author was ever more blessed.

CPSIA information can be obtained
at www.ICGtesting.com
Printed in the USA
BVHW030833191020
591324BV00004B/88